CHICAGO

COLORING
BOOK

During the 1920s and 1930s, the Chicago Transit Authority hired many talented graphic artists to create posters featuring parks, beaches, museums, universities, and other interesting locations inside and outside the Chicago city limits. These posters encouraged people to use public transit—called the elevated lines or 'L'—to travel to these destinations. The posters rarely depicted the 'L' itself; instead they displayed colorful and exciting images of buildings, cultural events, and outdoor activities.

Full-color reproductions of twenty of these posters are printed on the inside front and back covers of this coloring book, and line drawings based on the posters are included so that you can color them in. When you fill in the drawings, you might want to copy the original colors, or you might choose your own color combinations. We've left the last three pages of the book blank so that you can create pictures of your own. Can you draw and color your favorite museum, park, or building?

All of the posters included in this coloring book are from the collection of Poster Plus Publications, which offers the most extensive selection of vintage Chicago poster art ever reproduced.

Pomegranate **kids**®
AGES 3 to 103!

1. Willard Frederic Elmes, "Art Institute by the Elevated Lines," c. 1924. This poster depicts one of the two bronze lions flanking the Michigan Avenue entrance of the Chicago Art Institute.

2. Leslie Ragan, "Chicago: New York Central Lines," 1929. This poster features world-famous Michigan Avenue and a tourist standing near a peristyle admiring Chicago's iconic skyline.

3. Ervine Metzl, "Evanston Lighthouse by the Elevated Lines," 1923. Promoting travel to the outskirts of the city on the 'L,' this poster depicts a lighthouse on the lakeshore in Evanston, a town just north of Chicago.

4. Willard Frederic Elmes, "Golf by the North Shore Line," 1923. Featuring a female golfer, this poster promotes travel on the North Shore Line—an interurban railway that operated between Chicago and Milwaukee until 1963.

5. Oscar Rabe Hanson, "The Lake Shore by the North Shore Line," 1923. This image of seagulls skimming along Lake Michigan on a perfect Chicago day was created to promote travel along one of the last of the interurban railroads connecting Chicago and Milwaukee.

6. Oscar Rabe Hanson, "University of Illinois School of Medicine by the Elevated Lines," 1923. This is one in a series of posters designed to promote travel on the elevated lines to Chicago institutions of higher learning and cultural institutions.

7. Norman Fraser, "World's Fair Chicago: Travel Canadian Pacific," 1933. This dynamic and colorful image promotes travel to the 1933 Chicago World's Fair by way of the Canadian Pacific Railway.

8. After Arthur A. Johnson, "Avoid Street Congestion: Chicago Transit Authority, Loop 'L' Centennial," 1926. This popular poster captures the vitality and energy of Chicago's Loop; it was modified and republished in 1997 by special request from the Chicago Transit Authority for its 100th anniversary.

9. Ivan V. Beard, "Autumn in the Dunes by South Shore Line," 1928. One in a series of transit posters promoting travel on the South Shore Line Railroad, this image depicts golden-leaved birch trees growing in the lakeside dunes.

10. Oscar Rabe Hanson, "Chicago Civic Opera by the Elevated Lines," c. 1924. Featuring a magnificent image of the opera *Aida*, this poster promotes travel on the elevated lines to the Chicago Civic Opera House—the second-largest opera house in North America.

11. Willard Frederic Elmes, "The Lake Along the North Shore Line," 1924. Elmes designed this beautifully rendered poster to promote travel on the North Shore Line along Chicago's lakeshore.

12. Weimar Pursell, "Chicago World's Fair: A Century of Progress, 1833–1933," 1933. This poster promoting the 1933 Chicago World's Fair features the Art Deco–style Hall of Science. The fair focused on scientific and technological progress and the manufacturing processes behind them, hence the motto: "Science Finds, Genius Invents, Industry Applies, Man Adapts."

13. Oscar Rabe Hanson, "McKinlock Campus: Northwestern University by the Elevated Lines," 1923. Shortly after this poster was created, Chicago businessman George McKinlock suffered a financial loss; consequently he requested that his name be removed from the prospective downtown Northwestern University campus.

14. Arthur A. Johnson, "Summer Opera: Ravina Park by the North Shore Line," 1925. This poster, created to promote the Chicago North Shore and Milwaukee Railroad, depicts Giacomo Puccini's iconic opera *Madame Butterfly*. Note the misspelling of Ravinia Park in the poster caption.

15. Glen C. Sheffer, "World's Fair—Spirit of Chicago," 1933. Through the use of bright colors and dynamic lines, this poster illustrates the excitement and vitality of the 1933 Chicago World's Fair.

16. Arthur A. Johnson, "The Beaches by the Elevated Lines," 1923. In this poster, a lifeguard mans his post on one of the many sandy beaches that stretch along Chicago's lakeshore.

17. Raymond Huelster, "Spring in the Dunes by South Shore Line," 1928. Promoting travel on the South Shore Line, this poster celebrates the springtime beauty of the Indiana dunes.

18. Willard Frederic Elmes, "Chicago Civic Opera by the Chicago Rapid Transit," 1923. An image of Bizet's opera *Carmen* is used on this poster to promote travel on Chicago's elevated lines.

19. Ervine Metzl, "Field Museum by the Elevated Lines," 1923. This poster was designed to promote travel to Chicago's Field Museum of Natural History, which holds a fantastic display of dinosaurs and flora and fauna from around the world.

20. Oscar Rabe Hanson, "University of Chicago by the Elevated Lines," c. 1923. One of a series promoting travel on the 'L' to educational and cultural institutions, this poster depicts the University of Chicago, which is located in the southeast side of the city, near the lakefront.

Pomegranate Communications, Inc.
Box 808022, Petaluma CA 94975
800 227 1428   www.pomegranate.com

Color reproductions © 2012 Poster Plus • www.posterplus.com
Line drawings © Pomegranate Communications, Inc.

Catalog No. CB145

Designed and rendered by Gina Bostian and Stephanie Odeh

Printed in Korea

21 20 19 18 17 16 15 14 13 12   10 9 8 7 6 5 4 3 2 1

Distributed by Pomegranate Europe Ltd.
Unit 1, Heathcote Business Centre, Hurlbutt Road
Warwick, Warwickshire CV34 6TD, UK
[+44] 0 1926 430111
sales@pomeurope.co.uk

This product is in compliance with the Consumer Product Safety Improvement Act of 2008 (CPSIA). A General Conformity Certificate concerning Pomegranate's compliance with the CPSIA is available on our website at www.pomegranate.com, or by request at 800 227 1428. For additional CPSIA-required tracking details, contact Pomegranate at 800 227 1428.

1. "Art Institute by the Elevated Lines"

2. "Chicago: New York Central Lines"

3. "Evanston Lighthouse by the Elevated Lines"

4. "Golf by the North Shore Line"

5. "The Lake Shore by the North Shore Line"

6. "University of Illinois School of Medicine by the Elevated Lines"

7. "World's Fair Chicago: Travel Canadian Pacific"

8. "Avoid Street Congestion: Chicago Transit Authority, Loop 'L' Centennial"

AUTUMN IN THE DUNES BY SOUTH SHORE LINE

9. "Autumn in the Dunes by South Shore Line"

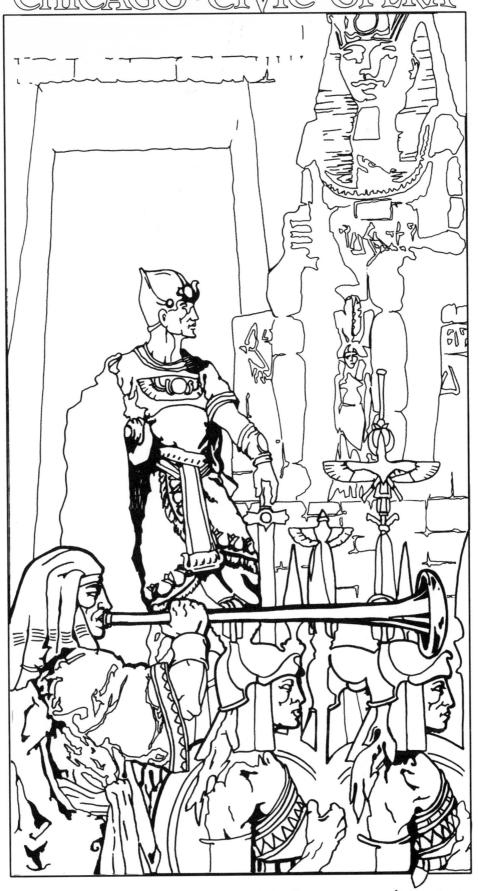

CHICAGO · CIVIC · OPERA

BY THE ELEVATED LINES

10. "Chicago Civic Opera by the Elevated Lines"

11. "The Lake Along the North Shore Line"

12. "Chicago World's Fair: A Century of Progress, 1833–1933"

13. "McKinlock Campus: Northwestern University by the Elevated Lines"

14. "Summer Opera: Ravina Park by the North Shore Line"

15. "World's Fair—Spirit of Chicago"

16. "The Beaches by the Elevated Lines"

17. "Spring in the Dunes by South Shore Line"

18. "Chicago Civic Opera by the Chicago Rapid Transit"

19. "Field Museum by the Elevated Lines"

20. "University of Chicago by the Elevated Lines"

Draw and color your own picture here!

Draw and color your own picture here!

Draw and color your own picture here!